Kendall & Tamara Schmitke
Illustrated by Rebecca Brebner

TWICE AS TIGHT

ISBN: 978-1-4866-0833-1

Word Alive Press
131 Cordite Road, Winnipeg, MB R3W 1S1
www.wordalivepress.ca

Library and Archives Canada Cataloguing in Publication

Schmitke, Kendall, 1975-, author
        Twice as tight / Kendall Schmitke (author), Tamara Schmitke (author) ; Rebecca Brebner (illustrator).

Issued in print and electronic formats.
ISBN 978-1-4866-0833-1 (pbk.).--ISBN 978-1-4866-0834-8 (pdf).--
ISBN 978-1-4866-0835-5 (html).--ISBN 978-1-4866-0836-2 (epub)

        I. Schmitke, Tamara, author II. Brebner, Rebecca, illustrator
III. Title.

PS8637.C44916T84 2015   jC813'.6   C2014-908113-8
                                                 C2014-908114-6

This book is dedicated to Donovan,
our precious son.

Our deepest thanks to Donovan's first mother,
who gave us a priceless gift.

Thanks also to our adoption agency,
Family Outreach International, for finding him
and to the people at International China
Concern who cared for him at his orphanage
until his 'gotcha' day.

"Whoever receives one such child in my name receives me."

—Jesus
Matthew 18:5, ESV

One drizzly morning, a sparrow hopped between the mud puddles. A heavy sack swung over her shoulder, and under her wing she clutched a tiny egg with a crack in it.

"Help!" she chirped into the forest. "Please help, our nest is broken!"

The only answer was the split-splat
of dripping leaves.

Then the egg shook by itself and the crack
spread. She eyed the crack in the egg and
cooed, "You need a nest to hatch in."

As the sparrow hopped along, she sang
this little song...

"I love you so much,
I must give you the best.
I'll find you a safe, healthy,
warm loving nest."

Soon she came across a lofty eagle nest. Two proud eagles were perched on the highest branch of the tree. One of them wore a velvety vest.

"There's a nest," the sparrow sang. "It looks strong."

But as she watched and thought, and thought
and watched, she finally turned away. "No, this nest
is not best. It is too high and those birds are so big.
You might get hurt."

So the sparrow hopped along and sang this little song…

"I love you so much,
I must give you the best.
I'll find you a safe, healthy,
warm loving nest."

Next she came across a cozy hummingbird nest.

Two hummingbirds zipped around a nearby bush, sipping nectar with their pointed beaks from trumpet-shaped flowers.

They wore wide-brimmed yellow sunhats that were tied beneath their chins.

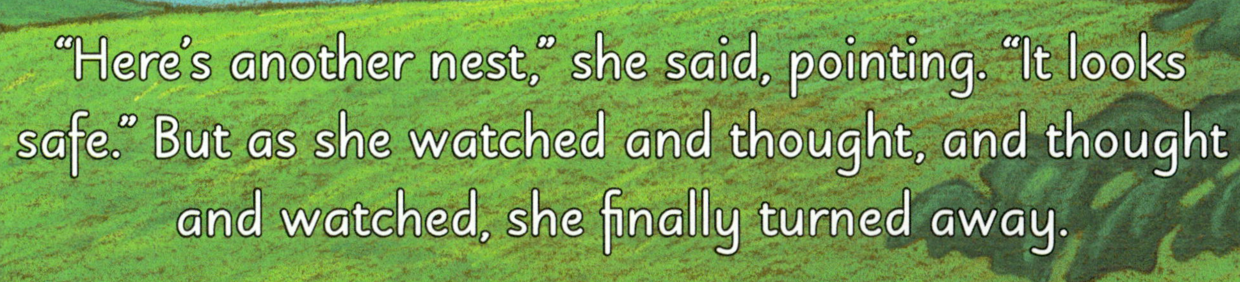

"Here's another nest," she said, pointing. "It looks safe." But as she watched and thought, and thought and watched, she finally turned away.

"No, this nest is not best. It is too small and their food is not enough for you. You might go cold or hungry." So the sparrow hopped along and sang this little song…

"I love you so much,
I must give you the best.
I'll find you a safe, healthy,
warm loving nest."

Next she came across a sturdy woodpecker nest. She heard the rat-tat-tat of a woodpecker echoing through the woods and spotted one wearing a striped necktie. "Here's another nest," she sighed, adjusting the sack over her shoulder. "It looks safe and healthy."

But as she watched and thought, and thought and watched, she finally turned away. "No, this nest is not best. Those birds are too busy. You might not be loved."

So the sparrow hopped along and sang this little song...

"I love you so much,
I must give you the best.
I'll find you a safe, healthy,
warm loving nest."

Then she came across a lively robin nest.
A mother robin wearing an apple-green
apron stood over the nest with a worm
dangling from her beak.

Three baby robins stretched their necks
upward, cheeping softly.

As the sparrow watched and thought, and thought and watched, her shoulders fell. "This nest might be best, but now I don't know if I can do this. It hurts my heart too much."

A tear rolled down her cheek and splashed onto the egg.

"I am so sorry that I cannot give you the nest you need," she whispered.

Just then, the little egg began to shiver and she heard a tapping noise inside. A tiny, yellow beak poked through.

The sparrow bent and tenderly
touched her baby's beak with her own
as a gentle lullaby drifted over them.

The robin was singing
to her babies and touching
each of their beaks with
her own, just like the
sparrow had done.

When the babies had quieted,
the robin whisked away.

The mother sparrow straightened and took a deep breath. "Yes. Now I know in my heart that this is the best nest."

She gently placed her egg in the robin nest. As she did, another tear splashed onto the baby's beak and she wiped it dry with her wing.

Before the sparrow hopped along,
she sang this little song…

"I love you so much,
I gave you the best.
I found you a safe, healthy,
warm loving nest."

With a mighty push, the baby poked its head
through the shell and squinted about.
The sparrow smiled proudly.

Snuggling her baby close, she whispered,
"Whenever they hug you, remember that I
am hugging you too."

"You will always be held twice as tight."